...Walking Along...

...Walking Along...

PLAINS INDIAN TRICKSTER STORIES

told and illustrated by
PAUL GOBLE

Foreword by ALBERT WHITE HAT, SR.

SOUTH DAKOTA STATE HISTORICAL SOCIETY PRESS / PIERRE

© 2011 by the
South Dakota State Historical Society Press
New material © 2011 South Dakota State
Historical Society Press
Text and illustrations © 2011 Paul Goble

All rights reserved. This book or portions thereof in any form whatsoever may not be reproduced without the expressed written approval of the South Dakota State Historical Society Press, 900 Governors Drive, Pierre, S.Dak. 57501.

The stories in this volume are condensed by Paul Goble from the following titles originally published by Orchard Books: *Iktomi and the Boulder* (1988), *Iktomi and the Berries* (1989), *Iktomi and the Ducks* (1990), *Iktomi and the Buffalo Skull* (1991), *Iktomi and the Buzzard* (1994), and *Iktomi and the Coyote* (1998).

The original artwork is used with the kind permission of the South Dakota Art Museum in Brookings, S.Dak.

This publication was funded, in part, by the Great Plains Education Foundation, Inc., Aberdeen, S.Dak.

Library of Congress Cataloging-in-Publication data
Goble, Paul.
Walking along : Plains Indian trickster stories / told and illustrated by Paul Goble ; foreword by Albert White Hat, Sr.
p. cm.
Includes bibliographical references.
ISBN 978-0-9845041-5-2
1. Indians of North America—Great Plains—Folklore. 2. Tricksters—Great Plains. 3. Tales—Great Plains. I. Title.
E78.G73G675 2011
398.2089'97079—dc23
2011022085

Printed in China

15 14 13 12 11   1 2 3 4 5

Foreword

I remember hearing Iktomi stories when I was a child. I imagined what he looked like, how he sounded, and how he walked. Iktomi's ability to trick just about any living being really awakened my imagination.

There was a lot to learn from the stories, too. The Iktomi storytellers use humor to teach about what happens when one uses trickery, lying, shrewdness, or underhanded actions against another creation, such as the ducks, the buffalo, and other relatives, as well as human beings. Sometimes people might want to do the same things that Iktomi does, but we learn from the stories not to do them.

Just like human beings, Iktomi has both a good side and a bad side. Some of the stories are silly, and a child will find them funny and entertaining. Other stories show Iktomi's evil side and have a tragic ending. Sometimes his actions are exaggerated, but that is only to make the moral of the story clear to the listener. As the child gets older and reaches maturity, these tales have a real meaning in life. If you study these stories, you will find Iktomi in you!

Lakota oral tradition includes a female trickster character, as well. Her name is Anog Ite, the double-faced woman. There are not as many stories about her, but women who dream about Anog Ite often become outstanding quill-workers.

For listeners or readers to understand the lessons of the tales, the stories must be told with Lakota thought and feelings. Iktomi calls the other creatures his "brothers." In Lakota culture, Inyan completed creation by joining his blood to create every being on earth, the grass, plants, land, ocean. When creation was completed, Inyan became dry and brittle and scattered over all the world—all my relatives. Iktomi stories teach us how we should treat our relatives, whether they are human, animal, other living things on the earth, or the earth herself.

I know Paul Goble has the understanding and wisdom to bring these lessons out in the stories, keeping the Lakota thought.

Albert White Hat, Sr.

. . . Walking Along . . .

Author's Note

Because every story about the American Indian Trickster starts with him "walking along," I have titled this book
   . . . *Walking Along* . . .
indicating that he is idle, directionless, easily distracted, always ready for the latest piece of fashionable nonsense or mischief. Like us, he is a complex and contradictory mix of evil, cleverness, and stupidity.

   In these stories, I have given the Trickster his Lakota name, Iktomi (pronounced *eek-toe-me*), which means spider. These Trickster stories are told all across the North American continent, although different people call him different names: Coyote (Crow), Sinti (Kiowa), Old Man Napi (Blackfeet), Nanabozo (Ojibwa), Sinkalip (Okanagan), Wihio or Ve'ho (Cheyenne), and many more. The details vary from one storyteller to another, but the themes, the ideas within the stories, are the same. I use the present tense because the Trickster is still alive in storytelling; nine times out of ten, when an American Indian tells a traditional story, it will be about the Trickster.

   Both Iktomi the spider and Iktomi the Trickster were here long before people, and being older, they are respectfully referred to as "Grandfather." If you kill a spider, you must say: "Grandfather Spider, the thunder beings kill you!" The spirit of the spider believes it is lightning that killed him, and he will not tell other spiders what you have done. In the Lakota language, it is *"Iktomi, Tunkashila, Wakinyan niktepelo!"*

The language of these stories is always colloquial because the Trickster has no respect for the finer points of grammar. The stories have an implied moral that is never spelled out as it is in Aesop's fables. Like most traditional stories, the Iktomi stories have deeper meanings that teach or provoke philosophical discussion. Today these stories are thought of as whimsical tales to entertain children, but in the old days, they were told only after dark to young and old alike. A person's faults and idiosyncrasies were likened to Iktomi's. A tipi village, which contained a small number of people, was a close-knit community. For everyone to live harmoniously, the community had to be well ordered and with high moral standards. Possibly these stories about the Trickster's wickedness were safety valves, giving voice to thoughts that were otherwise antisocial or taboo, a reminder *not* to be like Iktomi.

There is no "authentic" version of these stories. The only rule is that storytellers use certain themes and weave around them depending upon the audience. My stories emphasize an aspect of the Trickster that I feel is his most reprehensible: the way he takes advantage of the birds and animals, with their wondrous curiosity, innocence, and kindness, in order to kill them.

The stories are ancient; they seem more like pieces of almost-forgotten stories. Even the Trickster himself seems fragmentary and contradictory, being both a negative prankster and a divine helper of the Creator. Ella Deloria, a Lakota Indian who knew many of the old-time storytellers, wrote: "To our minds, [these stories] are a sort of hang-over, so to speak, from a very, very remote past, from a different age, even from an order of beings different from ourselves."

In the past, Iktomi was a mirror of human nature with its range of infinite possibilities. Now he has been relegated to his Trickster role, and his other aspects have been forgotten. People talk about "Iktomi Power" when they refer to the abuse of gambling, alcohol, or drugs, but it can also be power for good. In the beginning, Iktomi helped the Creator organize the world, gave people fire, tipis, bows and arrows, and all the necessary survival skills. Of course, he is also credited with the "mistakes" of creation, such as mosquitoes, flies, and earthquakes.

Over fifty years ago, I was sitting with Edgar Red Cloud in the shade of some cottonwood trees at the powwow ground at Pine Ridge, South Dakota, when he picked up a leaf and drew my attention to its shape. It had given Iktomi the idea for tipis, Edgar told me, and by folding the leaf, Iktomi had invented moccasins.

You cannot understand the Trickster with a scientific mind. He, like all of us, is more complex than we can ever figure out. He gives us the precious gift of laughter, and we should just enjoy him for who he is—for all his stupidity, pomposity, greed, vanity, laziness, wickedness, and any other negative human qualities you may wish to add!

Note to the Reader

There is no authentic version of the Iktomi stories. They have, however, always been told with audience participation. When the text turns to blue type, listeners are encouraged to make their own comments about Iktomi's antics. The text in small print, which are Iktomi's thoughts, may disrupt the flow of the stories. These comments can be read while looking at the pictures.

Iktomi and the Boulder

Iktomi was walking along. . . .
   *Every story about Iktomi
   starts the same way.*
Iktomi was going to visit his friends
and relations in the next village.
He was feeling happy with himself.
He had painted his face
and was wearing his very best clothes.

"How handsome I look," he thought.
"Everyone will be impressed.
 The girls will want me to notice them."
   *Iktomi is forever showing off—
   and then getting into trouble.*

My feather bonnet

My fan

I'm looking my
very best today.

I'll look great at the
dance tonight.

I bet the birds wish
they had all my feathers.

My tobacco bag

My blanket

The sun rose higher.
Iktomi was getting hot.
He had a long walk ahead of him.
His face paint started to feel sticky,
and wishing he had not put on
so many clothes,
he sat down to rest
in the shade of a great boulder.

"What a hot day!" Iktomi thought.
"Why did I bring my blanket?
I cannot be bothered to carry it any farther.

"Grandfather Boulder," he said,
"I feel sorry for you.
You are terribly sunburnt
from sitting here for so long in the sun.
You have given me shade.
I'm generous, too.
I give you my blanket to keep the sun off you."
He wasn't generous at all, was he?
Iktomi spread his blanket over the boulder
and went on his way.
"I'll pick it up on my way back," he thought.

After a while, he noticed dark clouds gathering.
"I might need my blanket after all,"
he said to himself as he walked back.
"Rain would spoil my clothes.
I did give it, though.
A gift is a gift. Still, . . . I need it.
Anyway, it's too nice to leave on a rock.

"Boulder," he said, "you don't need my blanket.
The sun can't burn you any more.
I was only lending it to you."
That's not true, is it?
Iktomi snatched the blanket off the boulder.

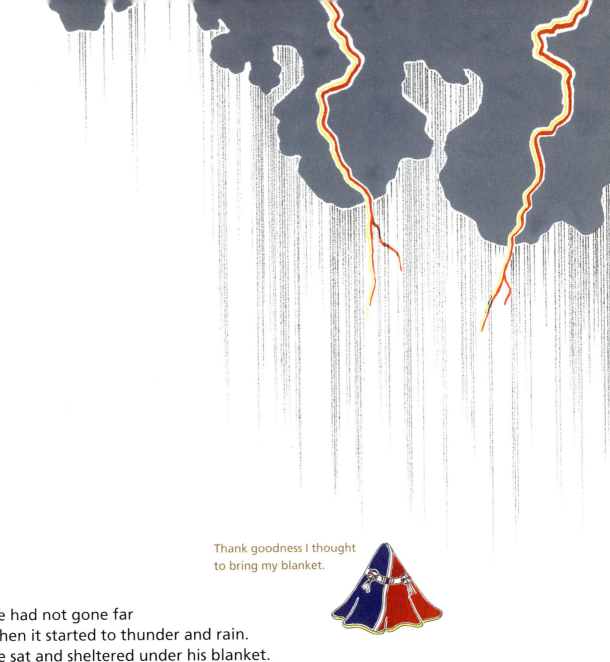

Thank goodness I thought to bring my blanket.

He had not gone far
when it started to thunder and rain.
He sat and sheltered under his blanket.
Soon, above the rumble of thunder,
he heard a different sound.
It seemed to shake the earth:
**thump–crash–bump–
thump–bump–crash.**

"That doesn't sound like thunder," Iktomi thought.
He peeped out from under his blanket;
that great boulder was bouncing
and crashing across the prairie
straight toward him!
He dropped his blanket and ran.

Anyone can outwit a rock!

"I must get to the top of the hill,"
he muttered in terror.
"The boulder cannot go uphill."
    He was wrong!
The boulder bounded end over end
right to the top.

"I must get across the river," he panted.
"That boulder will get stuck in the mud."
Iktomi ran toward the river,
the boulder bounding and thumping
close at his heels.
He ran this way. He ran that way.
He could not escape the boulder.

That rock has a terrible temper.

He splashed across the river.
Gasping for breath,
he scrambled out on the far bank
and fell down exhausted.

With one mighty bound,
the boulder jumped the river.
Before Iktomi could get up, it
rolled on top of his legs and stopped.
    Now what is Iktomi going to do?
He could not move.
He struggled. He screamed.
He hit the boulder. He pleaded. He cried.
The boulder did not move.

Some buffaloes heard him and came to look.
"My younger brothers," Iktomi said, "please help me."
    Iktomi has no respect.
    He calls everyone "younger brother."

"I was just climbing around on this boulder
when it rolled over onto my legs."
That wasn't true, was it?
"See, I cannot move. Roll it off me," he said.

The bulls got their horns underneath
and h-e-a-v-e-d and s-h-o-v-e-d,
but they could not move the boulder.
The elk and the antelope came to help.
Even the prairie dogs and the smallest
of the four-legged ones joined in,

What's the matter with you?
For goodness sake **push**!

but they could not roll the boulder
off Iktomi's legs.
They gave up and wandered off.
Darkness came, and bats appeared
with the rising moon.

"Ho! My younger brothers!"
 Iktomi called out to the bats.
"This boulder has been saying rude things.
 He said you are so ugly that
 you don't dare show yourselves
 during the daytime.
 He said that you sleep upside-down
 because you don't know your 'up side'
 from your 'down side.'
 He said some other things,
 but I simply cannot repeat them."
         Iktomi is making up stories, isn't he?
 It made the bats cross.

"I told the boulder he ought
 to know better than to insult
 his good-looking relatives.
 He even said that you don't know
 whether you are birds or animals,
 two-legged or four-legged.
 'Furry birds,' he called you.
 What a dreadful thing to say!"

Ha! That's done it!
I always knew I could get even
with that stupid rock.

The bats were furious.
They started hitting the boulder.
They darted this way and that,
and each time they struck,
pieces of the boulder broke off.

"Yes! *Furry birds* he called you,"
Iktomi shouted.

Bats and pieces of rock
flew in every direction.

"Don't know your 'up side'
from your 'down side'!"

The bats swooped at the boulder
until nothing was left but little chips.

"That's right." Iktomi told the bats.
"You taught that boulder a lesson."

Now let me think:
What shall I do now?

Iktomi went on his way again.
*What do you think he will
get up to next?*

*This story explains why bats
have flattened faces and
why rocks are scattered
all over the Great Plains.*

Iktomi and the Berries

Iktomi was walking along. . . .
 *Remember: every story about
 Iktomi starts the same way.*
He was out hunting. He said to himself:
"I'll shoot some prairie dogs and give
all my friends and relations a feast.
That will impress them!
'Ikto,' they'll say, 'you're a great hunter.
You're so generous; we love you.'"
 *Iktomi thinks a lot of himself.
 He is forever boasting about
 something he is going to do.*

Today I'm going hunting
in the old traditional way.

My ancestors knew a thing
or two about hunting—so do I.

My wig

My quiver of arrows

Coil of rope for tying up meat

My strike-a-light bag

My skinning knife

My ash-wood bow

My coyote-skin disguise

Iktomi was wearing a coyote skin.
"When I put this on," he said,
"the birds and animals think I'm
just another old coyote."

He doesn't look much like one, does he?

Iktomi stalked about with an arrow ready
against his bowstring.
He looked this way . . . and that way.

*He never noticed that the
prairie dogs were laughing at him!*

Iktomi was hot, thirsty, and very hungry.
His insides rumbled and grumbled at him:
"Ikto, you really must give us something to eat."

"Be quiet," Iktomi replied. "How can I hunt
if you make that noise?"

Do I look all right?
I'm not over-dressed, am I?
Why didn't I wait for
my wife to cook my
breakfast?

Is it duck season?

"This isn't any good," he thought. "Just when you want something, you can never find it. I'll go to the river and hunt ducks instead." Iktomi crawled cautiously toward the river.

What happened? Who pushed me?

Closer and closer he came.
He could hear the ducks talking.
> *Do you think they, too, are watching him and laughing?*

Iktomi never saw that the bank overhung the water.
It broke under him, and he fell in with a terrific splash.
All the ducks flew away.

Dripping wet, he sat beside the river,
totally disgusted and still hungry.
Just then he spotted some beautiful
red berries in the water.

"Ah! Fresh fruit. That's better!
That's exactly what I've been looking for."
    Is that true?
"I'll make berry soup.
My relatives will like that best of all.
'Ikto,' they'll say,
'we just *love* your berry soup.'
I'll get some ducks tomorrow."
    Do you think so?

"Ha!" cried Iktomi.
"Berries can't get away from me."
And with that he jumped into the river.
He felt around in the water.
"Where are they?" he asked.
He climbed out and
looked down into the water.
"Yes! There they are."
He jumped in again.

Just watch this fancy dive!

No berries. . . .

"I must have the wrong place,"
 Iktomi sighed as he climbed out.
"No! There they are! How silly of me
 not to have seen them.
 Third time lucky! Here goes!"
 Iktomi dived straight down to the bottom—
 and got his mouth full of mud.

"Everything is going against
 me today," he complained. "If I
 could just stay down longer. . . .
 I've got an idea! Yes, that's it!"
 Iktomi took his coil of rope
 and tied one end around his neck.
 He tied the other end around
 the largest rock he could lift.

"This rock will keep me down longer,"
 he thought to himself.
"Those berries won't get away now."
 He took a deep breath and swung the rock:
"One . . . two . . . THREE . . . "
 and was jerked off the bank after it.
        That was a stupid idea, wasn't it?

Imagine berries
growing in the water.
Oh, the wonders of nature!

The rock sank down,
dragging Iktomi to the bottom.
"This is better," he thought.
He groped around
on the riverbed until
he had to come up for air.

Where's my wig?
I've lost my leggings.

Oh, poor Ikto. . . .
What a way to die!
What *will* people think?

But he had forgotten the rock
tied around his neck.
He tried lifting it, but he couldn't.

"Rock, let go of me!" Iktomi said
He fumbled with the knot in utter panic.
"Oh HELP!"
    Does this look like the end of Ikto?

Anyway, I bet those berries were sour.

Iktomi was just about dead
when he floated to the surface.
He crawled out, gasping for air.
Exhausted, he turned on his back.
"That's odd," he thought.
He was looking up at the berries
in the bushes above his head!
All the while he had been seeing
their reflection in the water.
"Oh no! I hope nobody saw me."

Iktomi snatched up his bow
and set about beating the bushes.
"Take that!—and *that*—and THAT!
Don't you ever dare to try and
trick me like that again!
From now on, people will beat you
when they pick your berries."

Iktomi was so angry that he
knocked all the berries
off the branches.
They floated off
down the river,
and the ducks
had a fine
feast.

Let me think:
What was I going to do?
Oh yes, I'm hungry.
I'll get a hamburger, . . .
nothing to drink.

*That was a day Iktomi
does not wish to remember.*

Iktomi went on his way again.

Iktomi and the Ducks

Iktomi was walking along.
He was looking for his horse.
"I'll lead the parade," Iktomi thought.
"Everybody will notice me.
'Look,' they'll say to their children,
'yonder rides our War Chief,
the bravest of the brave.'"
Iktomi always thinks he is so great.
He could not see his horse anywhere.

I really do like myself.
I look like one of the old-timers.

I bet the girls will want to ride with me.

My otter fur (imitation) necklace

My red silk shirt

My beaded cuffs

My trade-cloth leggings

My moccasins

Iktomi noticed some ducks enjoying
themselves on a pond.
"Hmmmm . . . roast duck," he thought.
Iktomi always thinks about food.
"If I could just get hold of those ducks. . . ."

He hid behind some bushes
and broke off a thick branch.
What does he want that for?
Iktomi pulled up handfuls of grass
until he had collected a great pile.
He wrapped it together with
the branch inside his blanket.
He swung the bundle on his back
and walked briskly along
the edge of the pond.

I can fool ducks.
Watch me.

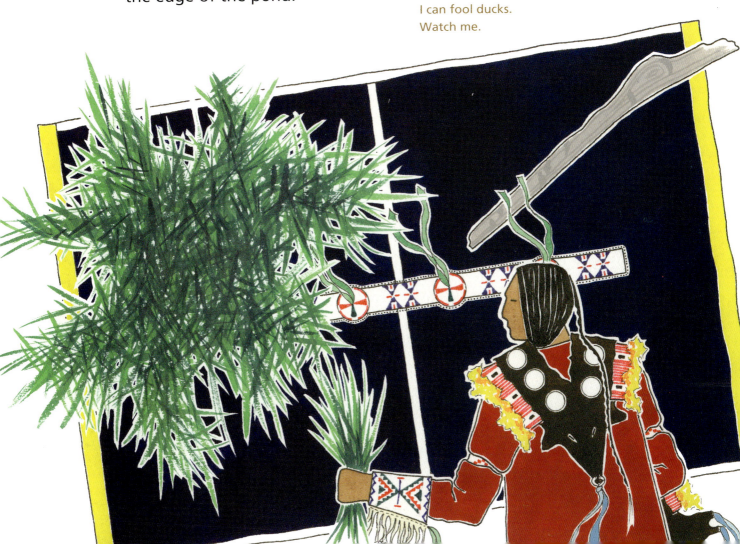

He pretended to be in a hurry,
rubbing the sweat off his forehead.

"Hey! Ikto!" the ducks called.
"What have you got in your blanket?"

"It's full of my latest songs," Iktomi told them.
"I'm off to sing them at the powwow."
Imagine carrying songs in a blanket!

"Sing us some, Ikto!" the ducks begged.

"Sorry," he said, "can't stop; in a hurry!"

"Oh please, PLEASE," they pleaded.

What else can I tell them?

These quack-quacks will believe anything I tell them.

"Well," he answered,
"all right, but only one."

The ducks swam to the shore
and waddled out onto the bank.
Iktomi felt inside his bundle
and drew out a single blade of grass.
"I'll sing this one," he said.
   Iktomi is up to mischief.

"Gather round. We'll all sing and
  dance together," Iktomi told the ducks.
"Now, this is a very special song.
  You must keep your eyes closed.
  If you open them, they will turn red.
  I'll beat time with my drumstick."
  He pulled the branch out of his bundle.
   He calls that a drumstick?

"Close your eyes!" he told the ducks.
"Now, dance while I sing:
>Close your eyes
>>and dance with me!
>Keep them shut
>>or they'll turn red.
>Close your eyes
>>and dance with me!"

Now we'll really have a powwow!

Ikto, you are *so* clever! You can call ducks off any pond!

Iktomi was beating time on the
ground with his branch.
"Dance! Stamp your feet!" he shouted.

The ducks joined in, eyes closed,
dancing with every bit of energy.
Suddenly, Iktomi started thumping
the ducks on their heads.
      Thump THUMP!—a duck was dead.
        Thump THUMP!—and another.
          Thump THUMP!—yet another.
One duck opened the corner of an eye
and saw what Iktomi was doing.

"Hey! Fly! IKTOMI IS KILLING US!"
The ducks took to the air in terror.
   Isn't Iktomi horrible?

Iktomi made a cooking fire.
He skewered the ducks on sticks
and put them around the fire to cook.
He buried one to roast in the ashes.
His mouth watered;
his stomach rumbled.

The wind started blowing.
The trees swayed from side to side.
Two trees scraped against each other.
"Creak! Cre-e-e-e-e-e-eak!"
"Squeak! Sque-e-e-e-e-eak!"
The sound got on Iktomi's nerves.

"Brothers shouldn't argue," he told them.
"You must stop, or I'll have to separate you."

When the trees took no notice,
Iktomi climbed up. Just as he
was pulling the trees apart,
the wind died, and he was
SQUASHED between them.

"What do you think you are doing? Let go of me!" he demanded.
"I AM IKTOMI!"

He struggled and he squirmed.
He wriggled and he wrenched.
He hit and kicked the trees,
but they held him prisoner.
It looks like the end of Iktomi, doesn't it?

Now Coyote had been watching everything.
You saw him, didn't you?
He trotted over to Iktomi's cooking fire.

"Go away!" Iktomi shouted.
"I won't give you anything."
When Iktomi saw that Coyote was
eating all his roast ducks, he pleaded:
"Leave me the one baking in the ashes."

Coyote turned his back so Iktomi
could not see what he was doing.
He uncovered the buried duck,
filled it with red-hot ashes,
and buried it again.
Coyote grinned and, licking his chops,
trotted on his way.

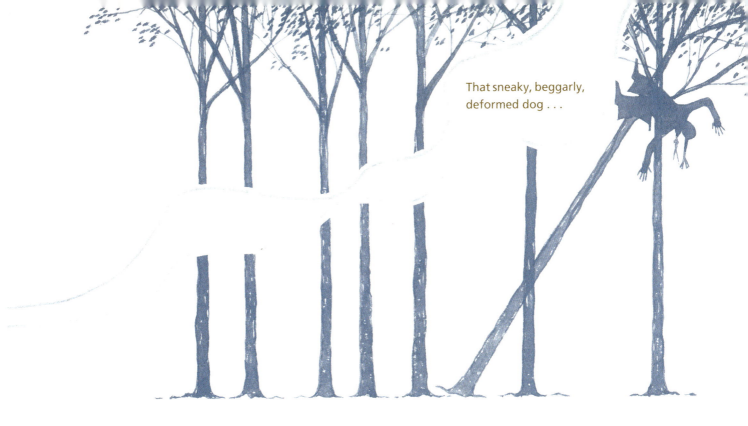

That sneaky, beggarly, deformed dog . . .

In a little while, the wind blew again,
and the trees let Iktomi go free.
He dug the duck out of the ashes.

"Thank goodness! Coyote left the best one,"
he muttered. He took a great hungry bite—
and got a mouthful of red-hot coals!

"AHRRRRRRR . . . . !!!!"

He jumped up and down,
spitting ashes in every direction.

"Just wait until I catch up with
that thieving Coyote.
I'll get even with him!"

Sore of mouth,
Iktomi went on his way again.

I never liked roast duck—
too greasy—bad for my
cholesterol level.
Now, let me think:
WHAT was I going to do?

Iktomi and the Buffalo Skull

Iktomi was walking along. . . . .
*Every story about Iktomi
starts the same way.*
He was wearing his best clothes.
He was going to get his horse.

I look good.

Yes, I'm looking very good indeed.

My warbonnet

My fan

My love-flute

I'm falling in love with my playing.

"It's a great morning!"
he was thinking.
"I'll ride over to the next village
and see my girlfriends."
   But Iktomi is already married!
"The girls will be impressed
with my new clothes.
'Hey! Just look at Ikto!' they'll say.
'I simply love Ikto!'
I'll pretend not to hear them
and perhaps they'll say
more nice things about me."
   *Iktomi always imagines that girls
   think he is so terrific.*

I'm a real traditional dancer.

At that moment he heard singing and
drumming. There was a dance somewhere!
He looked all around, but there was
nobody on the whole wide plain.
Iktomi's spirit stirred to the music.
The soles of his feet itched.
His moccasins began beating
up and down.
His eagle feathers moved and rustled,
and in a moment Iktomi was dancing
to the beat of the mysterious
singing and drumming.

When the song came to an end,
Iktomi sat down on a buffalo skull
to rest and to think. . . .
He jumped up with fright!
The singing had started again—
right underneath him!
It was coming from the buffalo skull!
He got down on his hands and knees
and peeked into an eye socket.
The Mouse People were having
a powwow inside the buffalo skull!

Are there mice inside my skull?

"Oh, Little Brothers," Iktomi said,
"you dance so gracefully.
Please let me join you."

"Oh no!" the mice replied.
"You are much too big.
You may put your head inside,
but *don't go to sleep!*"

Iktomi was just able to squeeze
his head into the skull,
but the singing made him sleepy.
> *Do you remember that the mice told
> him not to go to sleep?*

When the mice saw that he was sleeping,
they nibbled off his hair and
carried it away to line their nests.
When Iktomi awoke, his head
was stuck fast inside the skull.

Curses!

Iktomi could not see anything.
He had no idea where he was going.
He tripped and stumbled.
He got caught up in bushes,
and he fell into ravines.
    Iktomi is really in trouble, isn't he?
He crashed blindly into a tree.

"What tree are you?" he asked.
 I am Cottonwood," the tree replied.
"Ah! I must be close to the river."

Iktomi bumped into another tree.
"Friend, what tree are you?" he asked.
"I am Willow," the tree answered.
"Then I must be right beside the river,"
Iktomi said, and the next moment,
he stepped off the bank and
fell in with a mighty *SPLASH!*
Iktomi floated down the river.

When Iktomi heard voices,
he knew he had reached his village,
and he called out from inside the skull:
"Help! It's me! Come and help! Quick!"

People ran away in terror.
"A talking skull!" they cried.
"It's a spirit . . . a buffalo ghost!"

A few who were braver
threw their lariats over the horns
and pulled Iktomi from the water.
"Just look who we've got here!" they said.
"It's Ikto! Hey! Your wife has been looking
for you all day long. Better watch out!"

"Break this skull off my head,"
he gasped feebly.
His wife had her heavy stone hammer, which
she used for breaking marrow bones.

"You silly man," she scolded.
"You think I don't know where
you were going today? To see girls!
Do you think they wanted to see you?
You're a married man!"
With a WHACK, she struck the skull
with her stone hammer—
and it fell off in pieces.

Without much hair,
and with an awfully sore head,
Iktomi went on his way again.
*Who knows what he will
get up to next?*

My poor neck

Iktomi and the Buzzard

Iktomi was walking along. . . .
He was going to the powwow.
He was wearing feathers for the Eagle Dance.
"People like to see me Eagle Dancing,"
he boasted to himself.
"Sometimes I think I look just like Eagle.
Sometimes I think I look much better."

Iktomi is such a braggart!
He thinks so much of himself.

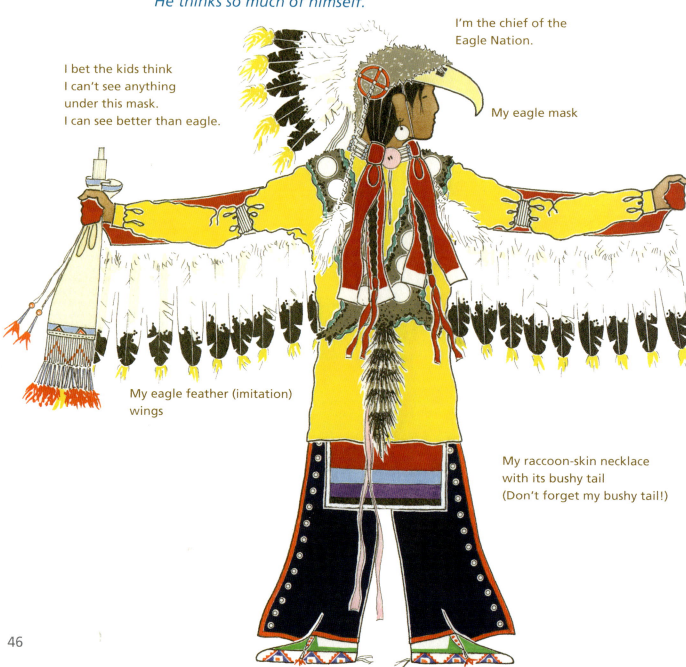

I bet the kids think
I can't see anything
under this mask.
I can see better than eagle.

I'm the chief of the
Eagle Nation.

My eagle mask

My eagle feather (imitation) wings

My raccoon-skin necklace
with its bushy tail
(Don't forget my bushy tail!)

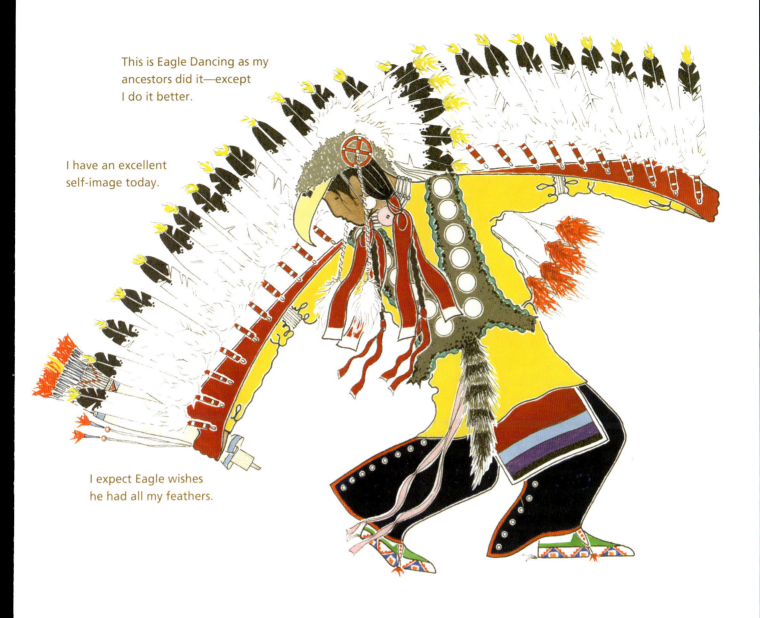

This is Eagle Dancing as my ancestors did it—except I do it better.

I have an excellent self-image today.

I expect Eagle wishes he had all my feathers.

Iktomi tried a few dance steps.
"I'm *Wanbli*, the Eagle.
See me soar above the buttes,
high up, close to Father Sun.
I look down on the whole world!
I glide over the plains.
Look at me everyone!"
    What imagination!
Iktomi came to a river too wide to cross.
Of course, he did not want to get
his feathers wet.

Iktomi sat down on the bank.
"Whatever shall I do now?"
My day was going so well.
Now I'll never get to the powwow.
I'll never win all the prize money."

Just then he spied *Hecha*, the Buzzard,*
making circles in the high above.
Buzzard sees everything moving below.
He had been watching Iktomi.
    You saw Buzzard, didn't you?

Iktomi pretended to cry,
but he was watching Buzzard's
reflection in the water.
In between his tears, he sang:
    "I am forever thinking: If only—
      if only I could reach the other side!"

TO'-KIN KO-WÁ-KA-TAN MA-KÁ-NI, E-CHIN'CHIN NA-WÁ'-ZHIN!
I STAND, THINKING OFTEN, OH THAT I MIGHT REACH THE OTHER SIDE!

*Turkey vulture—*Cathartes aura*

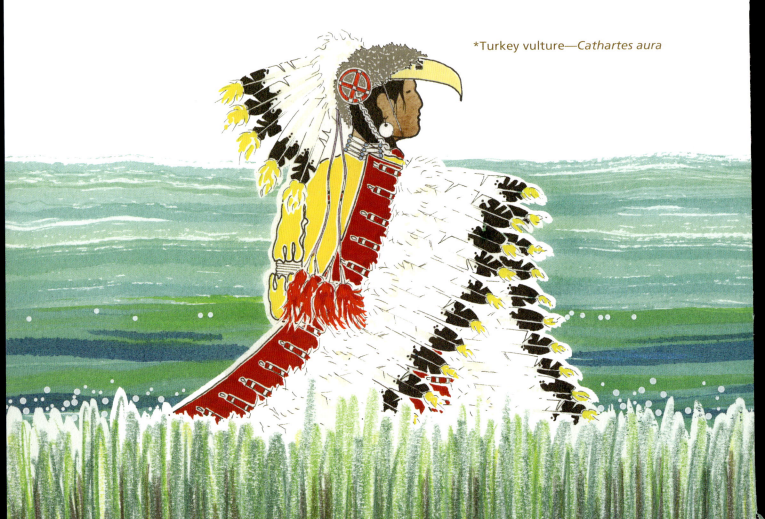

He sounded *so* terribly sad.
> *Those aren't real tears, are they?*
> *Iktomi must be plotting something.*

Iktomi sang the song again and again.

Buzzard circled lower and asked:
"Whatever is the matter? Don't cry."

"Ah! Hello, younger brother," Iktomi called.
"You gave me a fright! I didn't see you there."
> *That Iktomi is always telling lies.*

"My dear younger brother, I know it would grieve you to see me get my feathers wet. Therefore, would you, please, be so very kind as to transport me across this fluently flowing effusion of fluidity— this river?"
> *What language! How polite Iktomi is— when he wants something!*

"Yes, of course, older brother," said good-natured Buzzard.
"Get on my back, and I will carry you to the other side."

Iktomi once had lessons from a medicine man, and so he knew how to make himself smaller. He climbed onto Buzzard's back and sat astride his shoulders.

I bet the kids want to make this rude sign!

He's only a bird. He believes anything I tell him.

Thank goodness Buzzard can't see me!

I'm really on top of everything today.

"Now take me up high.
I want everyone to see
that I can fly," he told Buzzard.
He's wanting to show off as usual.
At that moment, Iktomi noticed that Buzzard
did not have any feathers on his head.
"Not a single feather!" he thought.
"Just red skin!"

Iktomi was so amused
that he almost fell off laughing.
He made rude signs behind Buzzard's head.
"Old baldy red skin!" he chuckled to himself,
and thinking he could not be seen,
he made insulting gestures at Buzzard.
*Do you think Buzzard knows what
Iktomi is up to?*

Buzzard sees everything that
moves on the earth below him.
Remember?
Buzzard saw what Iktomi was doing.
"The scoundrel," Buzzard said.
"I should have guessed.
I'll have my revenge on the rascal."

The birds saw Iktomi falling.
"Oh, look! It's poor Ikto!"
they chittered and chattered.
"Do something somebody!"

Iktomi fell inside the hollow tree.
He was still alive, but stuck fast.
Is this where he dies?

What a horrible way to die.

"My poor bones will lie here.
 Nobody will know my grave."
 Just then, Iktomi heard voices.
 Peering through a woodpecker's hole,
 he spied two girls with axes gathering firewood.
 He poked the bushy tail of
 his raccoon-skin necklace through the hole,
 and he sang in a high-pitched voice:
> "I'm a fat bushy-tailed raccoon,
> Sitting here, sitting here.
> Get me out, get me out,
> And you'll have lots of grease."

"Did you hear?" one of the girls asked.
"He says he's a fat raccoon. We need
 lots of grease for tanning hides."
 She pulled the tail, but Iktomi jerked it back.
 The girls chopped at the tree
 in time to Iktomi's singing.
 When it fell down,
 Iktomi clambered out.

"Whatever did you do that for?"
 he asked angrily.
"That was my house!"
 The girls ran away in fright.

 Laughing, and glad to be free,
 Iktomi went on his way again.
> *Can anyone guess what Iktomi
> will get up to next?*

Iktomi and the Coyote

Iktomi was walking along. . . .
We know by now that every story about Iktomi starts the same way.

I look like a real chief.
I AM a real chief.

My warbonnet and trailer (made of dyed domestic goose feathers)

My otter fur (imitation) necklace with mirrors

My book about me.

"Hi, I'm Iktomi. You know me.
Today I am going to the school
to read to the kids. I'll read them
these books that tell about
my brave deeds and generosity.
Everyone has read them.
I'm famous."

*Iktomi is famous, but it's not
for brave deeds or generosity, is it?
Do you think he can even read?*

"I'm wearing my traditional clothes.
The kids will see how the ancestors dressed
l-o-n-g, long ago,
although it has to be said:
I do look better than they did."
  Yes?
"I'll tell the kids how we lived in
Buffalo Days. I'm the only elder left."
  *Do you think he lived in those days,
  more than a hundred years ago?*

"What's that?"
Iktomi heard laughter
and high-pitched singing.

He looked this way—
and that way.
He could *not* see anyone.
Then he heard it again!

"Oh, look! It's the prairie dogs!
Hmmmmmmm. . . .
I'm real hungry for prairie dog!"
> *The only time Iktomi does not think about food is when he is eating!*

"There's nothing more tasty
than baked prairie dog."
> *Really?*

"Now, how shall I catch them?"

Iktomi crept stealthily toward
the prairie dogs.
They were playing a game,
taking turns being buried
up to their necks in the
hot ashes of their
cooking fire.
They were singing
a special song
that kept them
from getting
burned.

> I'm a great hunter—it's in my ancestral blood.

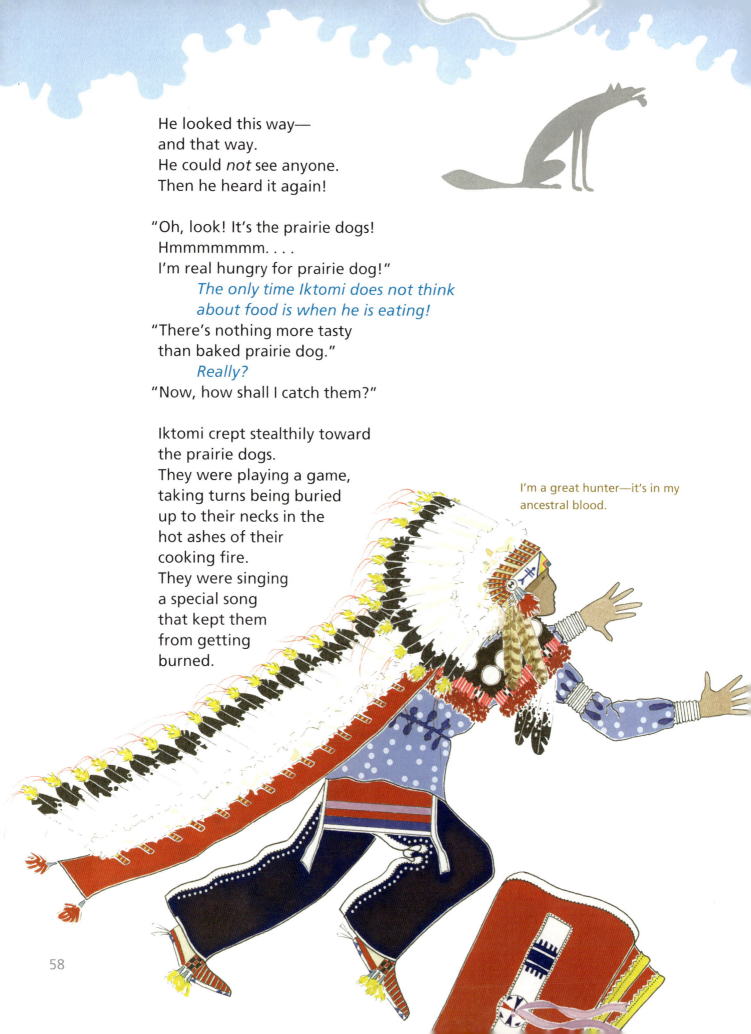

When the prairie dogs could not stand the heat any longer, they called out, and their friends quickly pulled them out. They were laughing and having so much fun.

"Oh my little brothers, what a great game," Iktomi said. Please bury me, too."

"Oh no, Ikto!" they all answered.
"You would *burn!*
First you have to learn our song.
Listen carefully to us!
Afterwards we'll bury you
in the ashes."
    Aren't prairie dogs kind?

"All right," Iktomi said,
"but I have an even better idea:
let me cover all of you with ashes,
all at the same time!
That way your song will be
so loud I'll be sure to hear it.
When you want me to
pull you out, just *shout* for *out!*"

"Oh Ikto, you have such
good ideas!" they said.
All the little prairie dogs quickly
lay down together, side by side,
like beans in a pod.

In a little while the prairie dogs
began crying to be pulled out, but
Iktomi just heaped on more ashes.
The prairie dogs implored him
to take them out.
One pleaded most piteously
for her babies soon to be born.
   You spotted her, didn't you?

"All right," Iktomi said,
 and he pulled her out.
"Go and live. Then there'll
 always be more prairie dogs."

After that, Iktomi hardened
his heart and closed his ears
to their screams . . . and
the prairie dogs baked to death.
   Isn't Iktomi horrible?

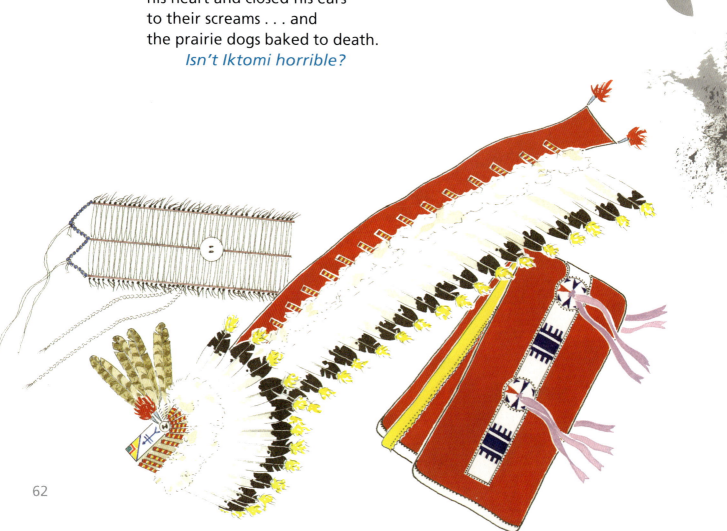

When Iktomi decided they
were well baked, he laid
them on willow twigs to cool.
He sat down on a rock.
His mouth was watering.
Just as he was going to
take his first bite, he caught sight
of Coyote approaching.
"I try, but I can never like Coyote,"
he muttered to himself.

Coyote looked very sad,
sick and starved, and he limped
slowly and painfully on three legs.
    We like Coyote, don't we?
"Oh Ikto, my older brother,
I'm feeling so weak," Coyote gasped.
"Please give me some of your meat.
I've had nothing to eat for so long."

"Certainly not!" Iktomi answered
hard-heartedly. "Not one single bite.
It's mine. *All of it.* Go away!"
But then Iktomi said, "Well, yes,
I'm a fair man."
    Hmmmmmm?
"I'll give you a chance. We'll gamble.
We'll race around that hill.
Winner eats all this meat."

Coyote's not my brother. I don't have to share NOTHING with him.

Fancy that silly Coyote thinking he could beat me!

"Ah, yes, my younger brother," Iktomi added, "I can see you are not in the best of health. To make it a fair race, I'll carry this rock." He put it in his blanket and slung it over his shoulder. Suddenly Iktomi called out, "1! 2! 3! Go!" and ran off as fast as he could, with the heavy rock bumping him at every step he took.

"Ikto! Wait! W-a-i-t," Coyote called, but Iktomi took no notice. "Ikto! Friend! Don't leave me."

When Iktomi was out of sight behind the hill, Coyote pulled off his bandages and rushed to eat the prairie dogs.
He had only been pretending to be sick!

When Iktomi came around the hill, he saw he had been tricked. "That's not fair," he panted. "You didn't leave me any. You didn't give me a chance."

Coyote replied: "I gave you as fair a chance as you gave the prairie dogs." Grinning and licking his chops, Coyote staggered off, feeling he had eaten too much.

"Just you wait," Iktomi warned. "You thieving, mangy good-for-nothing. I'll get even with you!"

Iktomi went on his way again.

Anyway, I never did like prairie dog meat.

Since then, prairie dogs' tails have had burned-black tips. They will never again trust two-leggeds or let them get close.

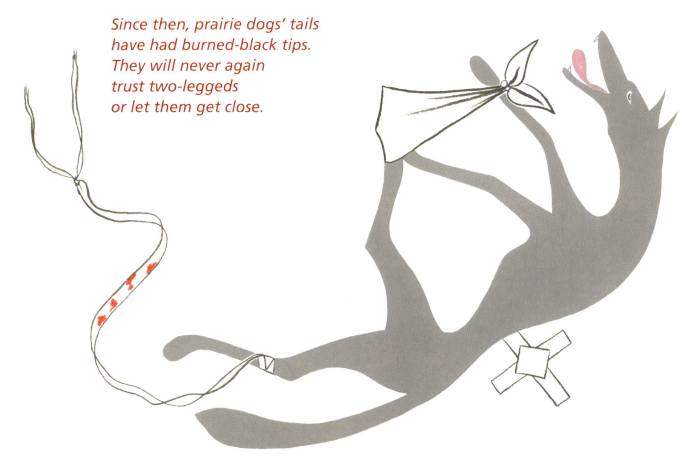

References
Maurice Boyd, *Kiowa Voices: Myths, Legends and Folktales,* vol. 2 (Fort Worth: Texas Christian University Press, 1983). Natalie Curtis, *The Indians' Book: An Offering by the American Indians of Indian Lore, Musical and Narrative, to Form a Record of the Songs and Legends of their Race* (New York: Harper & Bros., 1907). Ella Deloria, *Dakota Texts*, Publications of the American Ethnological Society, vol. 14 (New York: G. E. Stechert & Co., 1932). George A. Dorsey and Alfred L. Kroeber, *Traditions of the Arapaho,* Field Columbian Museum Publication 81, Anthropological Series, vol. 5. (Chicago: Field Columbian Museum, 1903). George Bird Grinnell, *By Cheyenne Campfires* (New Haven, Conn.: Yale University Press, 1926), and *Blackfoot Lodge Tales: The Story of a Prairie People* (New York: Charles Scribner's Sons, 1892). A. L. Kroeber, "Cheyenne Tales," *Journal of American Folk-Lore* 13 (1900): 161–90, and *Gros Ventre Myths and Tales*, Anthropological Papers of the American Museum of Natural History, vol. 1, pt. 3 (New York, 1908). Frank B. Linderman, *Indian Old-Man Stories: More Sparks from War Eagle's Lodge-Fire* (New York: Charles Scribner's Sons, 1920). Walter McClintock, *The Old North Trail; or, Life, Legends and Religion of the Blackfeet Indians* (London: Macmillan & Co., 1910). Sally Old Coyote and Joy Yellowtail Toineeta, *Indian Tales of the Northern Plains: Folk Tales from the Blackfeet, Sioux, Cheyenne, Crow, Flathead, and Arapahoe* (Billings: Montana Reading Publications, 1972). Vivian One Feather, *Ehanni Ohunkakan: A Curriculum Material Resource Unit* (Pine Ridge, S.Dak.: Red Cloud Indian School, 1974). Vince E. Pratt, *The Story of Iktomi (The Spider)* (N.p.: By the Author, 1988). Darnell David Rides at the Door, *Napi Stories* (Browning, Mont.: Blackfeet Heritage Program, 1979). John Stands in Timber and Margot Liberty, *Cheyenne Memories,* Yale Western Americana Series, vol. 17 (New Haven, Conn.: Yale University Press, 1967). Henry Tall Bull and Tom Weist, *Ve'ho* (Billings: Montana Reading Publications, 1971). R. D. Theisz, ed., *Buckskin Tokens: Contemporary Oral Narratives of the Lakota* (Rosebud, S.Dak.: Sinte Gleska College, 1975). Stith Thompson, *Tales of the North American Indians* (Bloomington: Indiana University Press, 1929). Clark Wissler and D. C. Duvall, *Mythology of the Blackfoot Indians,* Anthropological Papers of the American Museum of Natural History, vol. 2, pt. 1 (New York, 1908). Zitkala-Ša, *Old Indian Legends* (Boston: Ginn & Co., 1901).